Ladybird  Readers

The Talent
Show

Series Editor: Sorrel Pitts
Text adapted by Coleen Degnan-Veness
Illustrated by Ryan Wheatcroft

LADYBIRD BOOKS

UK | USA | Canada | Ireland | Australia
India | New Zealand | South Africa

Ladybird Books is part of the Penguin Random House group of companies
whose addresses can be found at global.penguinrandomhouse.com.
www.penguin.co.uk   www.puffin.co.uk   www.ladybird.co.uk

First published 2017
001

Copyright © Ladybird Books Ltd, 2017

Printed in China

A CIP catalogue record for this book is available from the British Library

ISBN: 978-0-241-29859-6

All correspondencwe to:
Ladybird Books
Penguin Random House Children's
80 Strand, London WC2R 0RL

MIX
Paper from
responsible sources
FSC® C018179
FSC
www.fsc.org

The Talent Show

talent show

Alex

Ziggy

band

dancers

Harmony School was the biggest school in Bridge Town.

One day, Mr. West said to the teachers, "Let's have a talent show. We need to find students who can sing, dance, or play music."

Soon, all the students knew about the Harmony School Talent Show.

"The Harmony School Talent Show starts tomorrow," said Mr. West.

Alex and the A-Stars were
a band.

"Let's try and win the
talent show!" said Alex.

Alex and the A-Stars practiced
their songs all day.

Ziggy and the Zigzags were dancers.

"We can win the talent show!"
said Ziggy.

Ziggy and the Zigzags practiced
their dancing all day.

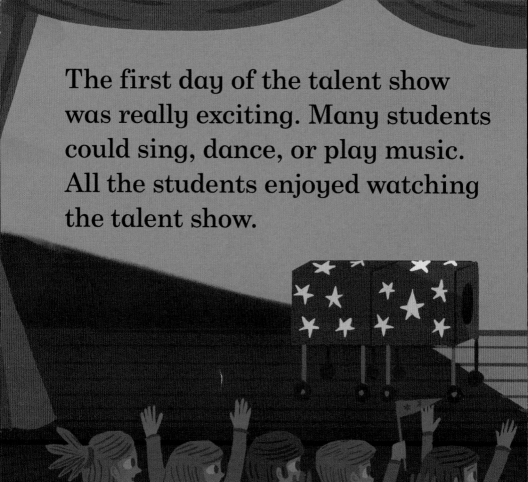

The first day of the talent show was really exciting. Many students could sing, dance, or play music. All the students enjoyed watching the talent show.

The A-Stars and the Zigzags
both did well on the first day.
All the students loved them!

"We're coming back tomorrow!"
Alex said to the A-Stars.

"We're coming back tomorrow!"
Ziggy said to the Zigzags.

The Zigzags practiced a new dance for the last day of the talent show.

"The Zigzags's dancing is great!" said Alex. "But we don't want them to win. We must work hard on our singing."

The A-Stars practiced a new song for the last day of the talent show.

"The A-Stars's singing is great!" said Ziggy. "But we don't want them to win. We must work hard on our dancing."

In the morning, Alex saw
Ziggy with his friends.

"Hello, Ziggy," said Alex.
"Your dancing is great,
but all the students love
my band's music more."

That afternoon, Ziggy saw Alex at school.

"Hello, Alex," said Ziggy. "Your music is great, but all the students love the Zigzags's dancing more."

It was the last day of the talent show. The A-Stars played their new song and all the students loved it. Then, the Zigzags danced.

Mr. West was ready to say the names of the winning students. All the students were excited.

"The Zigzags!" said Mr. West.

All the students were happy.

"Well done, Zigzags!" said Alex and the A-Stars.

The next day, Mr. West said, "The Bridge Town Talent Show is starting soon!"

All the teachers and students at Harmony School talked about it.

"We must try to win the Bridge Town Talent Show," Alex said to the A-Stars. "How about getting some people to dance with us?"

"We must try to win the Bridge Town Talent Show," Ziggy said to the Zigzags. "How about dancing to some new music?"

After school, Ziggy saw Alex.

"Hello, Alex," said Ziggy.

"Hello, Ziggy," said Alex.

"The A-Stars are great!" said Ziggy.
"We want you to play your music
with us."

"We love your dancing!" said Alex.
"We want you to dance with us!"

The A-Star Zigzags was their new name. The A-Stars played their music and the Zigzags danced to it.

Soon, all the students in the school talked about them.

41

The A-Star Zigzags wanted
to win the Bridge Town
Talent Show. They practiced
very hard together.

Soon, it was the first night of the Bridge Town Talent Show. The A-Star Zigzags played music, sang, and danced. Young people and old people liked them very much.

And who won? The A-Star Zigzags, of course!

Activities

The key below describes the skills practiced in each activity.

🖉 Spelling and writing

📖 Reading

💬 Speaking

❓ Critical thinking

✦ Preparation for the Cambridge Young Learners Exams

1 Look and read. Match the two parts of the sentences.

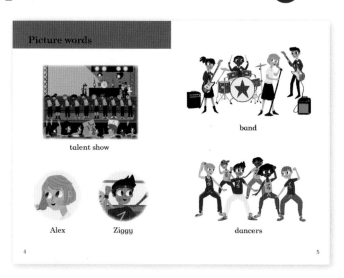

1 The girl who sings with her band is

2 The boy who loves dancing is

3 People who play music are in a

4 The dancers in the story are called

a Ziggy.

b band.

c the Zigzags.

d Alex.

2 Look and read. Write *yes* or *no*.

Harmony School was the biggest school in Bridge Town.

One day, Mr West said to the teachers, "Let's have a talent show. We need to find students who can sing, dance, or play music."

1 Harmony School was
in Bridge Town.   ......yes......

2 Harmony School was the
smallest school in town.   ....

3 Mr. West wanted to have a
talent show at the school.   ....

4 Mr. West spoke to the
teachers.   ....

5 A talent show needs
teachers who can sing,
dance, or play music.   ....

3 Circle the correct words.

1 Alex and the A-Stars
were / **are** a band.

2 "Let's **try** / **tried** and win
the talent show!" said Alex.

3 Ziggy and the Zigzags
were / **are** dancers.

4 "We can **win** / **won** the
talent show!" said Ziggy.

4 **Find the words.**

knibundlouwoik(band)ztalentshowmnuzdancerstrocmusic

> band
> talent show
> music
> dancers

5 **Look, match, and write the words.**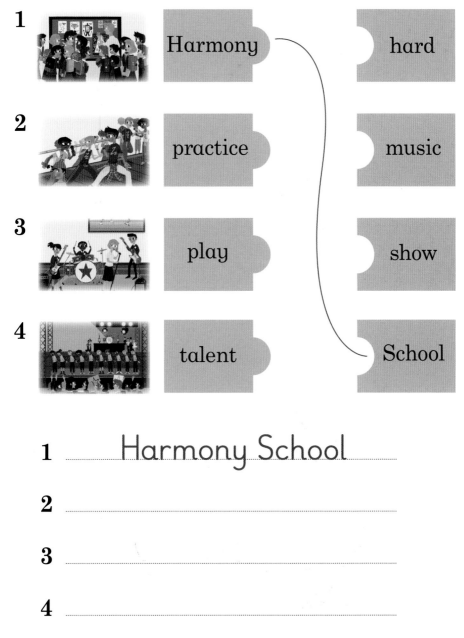

1   Harmony   hard

2   practice   music

3   play   show

4   talent   School

1   Harmony School

2

3

4

6 Ask and answer questions about the picture with a friend. 🗨 ❓

1 *How many dancers are there in the Zigzags?*

There are six dancers.

2 How many dancers are boys?

3 What are they wearing?

4 How old are the dancers, do you think?

7 Choose the correct answers.

Soon, it was the first night of the Bridge Town Talent Show. The A-Star Zigzags played music, sang, and danced. Young people and old people liked them very much.

And who won? The A-Star Zigzags of course!

1 Alex and the A-Stars were good at

  a dancing.

  b playing music.

2 Ziggy and the Zigzags were good at

  a dancing.

  b playing music.

3 The A-Star Zigzags had

  a good dancers.

  b good music and good dancers.

8 Read and circle the correct verbs.

1 The A-Stars and the Zigzags both **made** / **did** well on the first day.

2 All the students **loved** / **loves** them!

3 "We **are coming** / **came** back tomorrow!" Alex said to the A-Stars.

9 **Read the text. Choose the correct words, and write them next to 1—6.**

Alex	singing	dancing
Ziggy	hard	win

"The Zigzags's dancing is great!"

said ¹ _Alex_. "But we don't want

them to ² _____. We must

work hard on our ³ _____."

"The A-Stars's singing is

great!" said ⁴ _____.

"But we don't want them

to win. We must work

⁵ _____ on

our ⁶ _____."

10 Do the crossword. 📖 ✏️

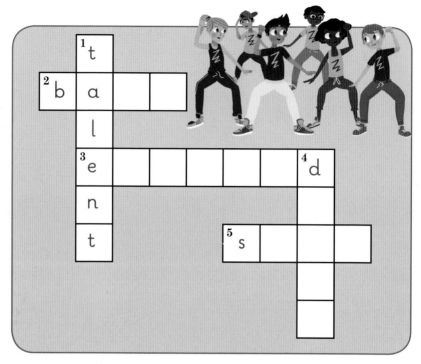

<table>
<tr><td>¹t</td></tr>
<tr><td>²b</td><td>a</td><td></td><td></td></tr>
<tr><td>l</td></tr>
<tr><td>³e</td><td></td><td></td><td></td><td></td><td>⁴d</td></tr>
<tr><td>n</td></tr>
<tr><td>t</td><td>⁵s</td></tr>
</table>

Down

1 Harmony School had a . . . show.

4 The Zigzags could . . . very well.

Across

2 Alex and the A-Stars were a . . .

3 All the students were . . .

5 The A-Stars could . . . very well.

11 Look at the pictures with a
friend. One picture is different.
How is it different? 🗨 ❓

1 ⓐ ⓑ ⓒ

Picture c is different
because they are dancing
rather than playing music.

2 ⓐ ⓑ ⓒ

3 ⓐ ⓑ ⓒ

12 **Look at the letters. Write the words.** 📖 ✏️

1 (n i w)

"We must try to _win_ the Bridge Town Talent Show," Alex said to the A-Stars.

2 (t e t i g n g)

"How about _____ some people to dance with us?"

3 (e a t n T l)

"We must try to win the Bridge Town _____ Show," Ziggy said to the Zigzags.

4 (n d i a n g c)

"How about _____ to some new music?" said Ziggy.

Write *Who*, *What*, or *Where*.

1 _____Who_____ did Ziggy
see after school?

2 _____ are Ziggy
and Alex? Are they in school?

3 _____ is Ziggy
thinking about? Is it Alex?

4 _____ did you see
the Zigzags dance?

59

14 **Read the answers. Write the questions.**

"The A-Stars are great!" said Ziggy.
"We want you to play your music
with us."

"We love your dancing!" said Alex.
"We want you to dance with us!"

1 <u>Who were dancers?</u>

Ziggy and the Zigzags
were dancers.

2 ....

Alex and the A-Stars were a band.

3 ....

The Zigzags won the Harmony
School Talent Show.

15 **Read the questions. Write the answers.** 📖 ✏️ ❓

1 What did the A-Stars think when they saw the Zigzags practicing?

They thought they must practice their singing.

2 How did the A-Stars feel when the Zigzags won the Harmony School Talent Show, do you think?

....

....

3 Were Alex and Ziggy friends, do you think?

....

....

16 **Talk to a friend about the A-Star Zigzags.** 💬 ❓

> 1 *Were the A-Stars as good as the Zigzags?*

> *No, they weren't. The Zigzags won the Harmony School Talent Show.*

2 Why did Alex and Ziggy want to work together?

3 Was it a good idea for the A-Stars and the Zigzags to work together?

4 What did the people in Bridge Town enjoy most in the talent show?

5 Would you like to be in the A-Star Zigzags?

17 Write about your favorite band or dancers. Why are they your favorite? ✏️ ❓

My favorite

Level 3

Sharks

978–0–241–25382–3 ☐

The Jungle Book

978–0–241–25383–0 ☐

The Red Knight

978–0–241–25384–7 ☐

The Elves and the Shoemaker

978–0–241–25385–4 ☐

Rapunzel

978–0–241–28394–3 ☐

Great Buildings

978–0–241–28400–1 ☐

Minibeasts

978–0–241–28404–9 ☐

Puss in Boots

978–0–241–28407–0 ☐

Jack and the Beanstalk

978–0–241–28397–4 ☐

Hansel and Gretel

978-0-241-29861-9 ☐

The Talent Show

978-0-241-29859-6 ☐

A Great Night!

978-0-241-29863-3 ☐

Bumblebee and the Rock Concert

978–0–241–29867–1 ☐

Where Animals Live

978–0–241–29868-8 ☐

Now you're ready for Level 4!